Alex sighed. She and
There was nothing more they could do. She would
let God and Mrs. Tuttle decide which was the best
project.

Finally, on Thursday morning, Mrs. Tuttle said,
"I have decided which project should represent our
class at the fair."

The class was completely quiet. Mrs. Tuttle
paused. The children sat on the edges of their seats.
Alex held her breath.

"The name of the project that will go to the
Social Studies Fair is—"

ALEX

Hot Chocolate Friendship

Nancy Simpson

Chariot Victor Publishing
A Division of Cook Communications

Chariot Victor Publishing
A division of Cook Communications, Colorado Springs, Colorado 80918
Cook Communications, Paris, Ontario
Kingsway Communications, Eastbourne, England

HOT CHOCOLATE FRIENDSHIP
© 1987 by Nancy Simpson for text and GraphCom Corporation for interior
illustrations.

Cover design by Megan Keane DeSantis
Cover illustration by Don Stewart

First printing, 1987
Printed in the United States of America
03 02 01 00 99   16 15 14 13 12

Library of Congress Cataloging-in-Publication Data

Simpson, Nancy, 1949-
Hot chocolate friendship
Summary: Alex is disappointed when she is assigned to do a social studies project
with Eric, the slowest student in the third grade.
[1. Schools-Fiction. 2. Friendship-Fiction.]
I. Dorenkamp, Michelle, ill. II. Title.
PZ7.L5724Ho 1987
[Fic]   87-5281
ISBN 078143257X

To the Holy Spirit
who fills page after page
with the very thoughts of God
and
To Cathy Daniels
who, filled to the brim
with love for others,
keeps pouring and pouring.

Dear friends, let us practice loving each other, for love comes from God and those who are loving and kind show that they are the children of God, and that they are getting to know him better.

I John 4:7
The Living Bible

CONTENTS

The ALEX Series
by Nancy Simpson Levene

- Shoelaces and Brussels Sprouts
- French Fry Forgiveness
- Hot Chocolate Friendship
- Peanut Butter and Jelly Secrets
- Mint Cookie Miracles
- Cherry Cola Champions
- The Salty Scarecrow Solution
- Peach Pit Popularity
- T-Bone Trouble
- Grapefruit Basket Upset
- Apple Turnover Treasure
- Crocodile Meatloaf
- Chocolate Chips and Trumpet Tricks
  —an Alex Devotional

CHAPTER 1

An Impossible Partner

"Pow! Pow! Pow! Got ya!" shrieked a hidden voice.

Alex looked up just in time to see the snowball an instant before it exploded in her face.

"Bam! Bam! Have another one!"

A second snowball streaked through the air hitting Janie's shoulder, splattering snow all over her and the schoolbooks she was carrying.

"Aaahhh!" the girls screamed and struggled to wipe the wet, cold snow off their faces, necks, and books.

"Goblin!" Alex screeched. "I'm gonna pulverize you!"

"Was that Rudy?" Janie asked. She shook white flakes out of her math book.

"Who else but Rudy and Jason?" Alex muttered. She had flung her backpack down on top of the snow-covered ground and was trying to reach an extra cold bit of snowball that had slipped under the collar of her coat and had worked its way down her back.

"Aw, brussels sprouts!" Alex tore off her coat and flopped it down beside her backpack. "Will you brush the snow off me?" she asked Janie.

Janie brushed off Alex's back, and Alex brushed off Janie's shoulder. Janie shook the snow out of her schoolbooks. Alex buttoned her coat and picked up her backpack.

"If we hurry, maybe we can catch those boys," Alex suggested. "I'll teach that little brat to throw a snowball in my face!"

"That little brat" was Alex's younger brother, Rudy. His real name was David, but he insisted that everyone call him Rudy. Everyone did but Alex. She usually called him *Goblin*.

Rudy was six years old and in first grade this year. That meant that Alex not only had to put up with him at home but also had to put up with him all day at school. She tried to ignore him whenever they met in the halls or at recess, but ignoring

Rudy was sometimes harder than clobbering him.

"There they are!" Janie pointed.

"Okay, quick! Let's catch them!" Alex replied.

The two girls hid behind bushes, trees, and parked cars as they quickly made their way down Juniper Street. When they neared the boys, they stopped and packed together several clumps of snow.

"CHARGE!" The girls swooped upon the two younger boys and let their snowballs fly. One hit the back of Rudy's neck and another skimmed the top of his head. Jason's back was hit and so was his left cheek.

The boys quickly made their own supply of snowballs. All the way to school, the white balls flew back and forth, hitting and missing their targets. At one point, Alex bravely stormed through the battle and flung Rudy into a snow-drift. She was rewarded with handfuls of snow tossed into her face.

By the time the children reached the school, they looked like four snowmen. Rudy and Jason scampered down a hallway to their first-grade room, while Alex and Janie stomped their way down another hallway to their third-grade room.

"It's Big Foot!" screamed a boy when Alex and Janie entered the classroom. "Yikes!" Several boys crawled under their desks to hide from the snow monsters.

"All right, children, let's quiet down," Mrs. Tuttle called to the class. She smiled at Alex and Janie. "It looks more like two Frostys have come to town than Big Foots."

"We got in a snowball fight with my dumb brother," Alex explained.

"I see," replied Mrs. Tuttle. "He must be quite a snowball fighter to cover both of you with so much snow."

"Not really," Alex told her. "You should see him. His teacher probably needs an ice pick to get him out of his jacket!"

Mrs. Tuttle laughed. "Go hang up your coats, girls. Class is ready to begin."

Alex whistled softly as she hung her coat in the coat closet. She was so glad to have Mrs. Tuttle for her third-grade teacher. Mrs. Tuttle was young and pretty and lots of fun. Not at all like

THE BULLDOZER. THE BULLDOZER had been Alex's second-grade teacher. Alex shuddered to think what THE BULLDOZER would have said if she had come to class covered from head to toe with snow.

When the children were all seated and quiet, Mrs. Tuttle said, "Because this is the last day before Christmas vacation, I know that you are all excited."

"Yea!" interrupted the class. It was three days before Christmas.

Mrs. Tuttle held up her hands. "I want to tell you about a special project we are going to do."

"Boo!" the class groaned. They didn't want to hear about a project. They didn't want to hear about anything that had to do with schoolwork. They were ready for Christmas vacation.

Mrs. Tuttle understood. She smiled and said, "We aren't going to work on the project until after the holidays. But I want you to be thinking about it."

Alex grumbled to herself, "Brussels sprouts, teachers always want you to think, even during Christmas vacation!"

13

"Each one of you will have a partner to work with on this project," Mrs. Tuttle explained.

Alex raised her hand.

"Yes, Alex?"

"May we pick our partners?"

"No, I have already picked the partners," answered Mrs. Tuttle. "I will tell you who they are in a few minutes."

Alex looked disappointed. She wanted Janie for her partner. She doubted that Mrs. Tuttle had chosen her best friend for her partner. Things didn't usually work out that way.

"Now," Mrs. Tuttle went on, "I am going to pass out a list of countries. You and your partner will choose a country from the list. You will then find out all about your country and write a report about it. You also need to make some kind of display—like a map or a poster or even a model of a famous building in your country."

As Mrs. Tuttle talked, she walked up and down the rows of desks, handing a piece of paper to each child. Alex looked at hers. "Argentina, Brazil, Canada, Denmark, Egypt, France . . ." Alex remembered reading about some of the countries from her social studies book.

"We will talk more about how to do the reports later," Mrs. Tuttle was saying. "Let me read the list of partners now."

Alex tensed. Who would be her partner? It was too good to hope for Janie. She just hoped she wouldn't get a boy as a partner. Especially not a bratty boy like Eddie Thompson.

"Maybe I should say a quick prayer," she told herself.

Mrs. Tuttle began calling out the partners' names. "Sarah Tomkins and Ronnie Barr, Randy Lewis and Lara Bruce, Julie Nettles and Janie Edwards . . ."

That lucky Janie, thought Alex. *She got a girl for a partner!*

"Eddie Thompson and Sally Wallace," continued Mrs. Tuttle. "Alexandria Brackenbury and Eric Linden . . ."

Alex heard no more of the list. She clutched the end of her desk and opened her mouth wide. "Eric Linden!" she almost shouted. Eric Linden was her partner? How could Mrs. Tuttle do that to her? Eric Linden was the worst student in the whole class. He couldn't even keep up with the last reading group. Brussels sprouts!

Mrs. Tuttle had finished her list. "Okay, everyone, meet with your partner and decide on a country," she said. "As soon as you have picked your country, let me know and I will write it on the blackboard. That way the rest of the class will know not to choose your country."

Chairs banged and desks scooted as the children scurried to find their partners. Alex did not move. She did not want to spoil the last day before Christmas vacation by having to talk to Eric Linden! Maybe her teacher wouldn't notice if she sat very quietly.

Alex sneaked a peek at Eric. He hadn't moved either. He was sitting still and staring at the top of his desk. "Well, why does he look so sad?" Alex grumbled to herself. "He ought to be glad to get me as a partner. I'm the one who should be sad!" She laid her head down on her desk.

"Alex," a voice said above her. "Why aren't you meeting with your partner?"

Alex raised her head and frowned at her teacher. "I'd rather not," she answered.

"Now, Alex," Mrs. Tuttle said in a low voice. "I am counting on you to help Eric with this project. He needs a good student as a partner—someone who can take charge and show him how to do the report. I think you are the best one for the job. Will you do it for him and for me?"

Alex stared at her teacher. She hadn't really thought about it in that way. And besides, Mrs. Tuttle was looking at her with such a warm smile and friendly eyes, how could she refuse?

"Okay," answered Alex with a shrug of her shoulders. She got up and carried her chair over to Eric's desk.

"Hi," she said as she sat down beside him.

Eric didn't answer. Alex wasn't surprised. Eric hardly ever spoke to anyone.

"Uh, we need to pick a country. What country do you want?" Alex asked without much hope of getting an answer.

Eric still did not speak.

"Okay, well, I guess I can pick the country," she said more to herself than to Eric. She began studying the list of countries and thinking out loud, just in case Eric decided to help. "Argentina, Brazil, Canada. . . . Hey, Canada might be good. We went there once for our vacation." Alex checked the blackboard. "Aw, too late. Somebody else got it."

She looked back at the list. "Japan would be neat. We could draw a picture of kids doing karate! Chop! Chop!"

Alex grinned at Eric. He squirmed a little and glanced sideways at her.

Well, at least he looked at me, thought Alex. *That's something.* She again checked the black-board. Japan had been chosen, too. "Brussels sprouts! I better cross off the ones that are on the blackboard so we can see what's left." When she had finished, there were only three countries available.

"I guess it's Brazil, India, or Spain," she told Eric. "No, there goes India and there goes Spain. I guess we get Brazil. What's in Brazil anyway?"

"Children," Mrs. Tuttle called to the class. "I would like for you to think about your country over vacation and try to come up with some ideas for your project. I will choose the best project to represent our class in the Social Studies Fair in February. Every school in our district will submit entries. It would be quite an honor to have your project chosen. Who knows? Someone from this class might even win the grand prize!"

The children's eyes sparkled as they grinned at their partners. It was exciting to think that they could win a prize.

Alex did not grin. She didn't even glance at Eric. The whole project seemed impossible to her. How could she do anything with a partner that wouldn't even talk?

CHAPTER 2

Christmas

"Alex! Wake up, Alex! I heard him! I heard him!"

"What? What's going on?" Alex sat up in bed and rubbed her eyes. A hand poked her shoulder.

"Alex, listen! Do you hear anything?"

"Goblin! What are you doing in here in the middle of the night?" Alex peered at the clock beside her bed. It was either 12:15 or 3:00. Her eyes were too fuzzy to tell the big hand from the little hand.

"I know he's down there," Rudy whispered in her ear.

"Who?" Alex almost shouted.

"Shhhh, he'll leave if he hears you," warned Rudy. "He's down there right now stuffing little toys and candy in our stockings."

"Santa Claus!" Alex exclaimed. She was wide awake now.

She rushed out of her bedroom with Rudy right behind her. She stopped at the top of the stairs and peered down.

A soft glow of light filled the bottom of the stairway. Alex looked excitedly at Rudy. Rudy grinned. They quietly crept down the steps to the bend in the stairway. On hands and knees, they slowly peeked around the bend into the living room below.

All was still and quiet. Alex could hear the steady tick of the old grandfather clock. She gazed at the Christmas tree as it merrily blinked red, green, blue, gold, and white.

"THERE HE GOES!" Rudy screamed so loudly that Alex lost her balance and tumbled down two steps before she could catch herself.

Rudy scrambled down the steps and bounded toward the fireplace.

"HE WAS RIGHT THERE, ALEX! I SAW HIS BOOTS! I SAW HIS BOOTS!" Rudy hopped up and down pointing his finger at the inside of the fireplace. "Quick! Outside! He might still be on the roof!"

Alex yanked open the front door and she and Rudy raced into the frosty front yard, their bare feet hopping through the snow. The stars twinkled and the moon winked as the children studied the roof, particularly the chimney area.

A loud voice broke the silence.

"Alex! Rudy! What are you doing out there?"

A man stood in the front doorway. He was not dressed in a red suit and red hat. He did not wear black boots, and he certainly did not have a snow-white beard. This man wore a green bathrobe and slippers. His brown hair stuck up in odd places.

"Hi, Dad," greeted Rudy as if it were perfectly ordinary to stand outside in the middle of the night, barefooted in the snow, wearing pajamas.

"Rudy and Alex, get in this house immediately!" Father ordered.

Both children hurried inside. They began telling their father about Rudy seeing black boots in the fireplace.

"Shhhh," Father told them. "You'll wake up the rest of the family."

"The rest of the family is awake," announced a voice from the top of the stairs.

Mother made her way down the stairway. Her blonde curls bounced against the top of her silvery blue bathrobe.

Alex's older sister, Barbara, stumbled down the stairs after Mother. Alex grinned. Poor Miss Mushy! Her sister would not sleep until noon this time. Seeing Miss Mushy awake at this hour was worth any trouble she and Rudy might get into for waking the family.

"What time is it?" Barbara grumbled.

"Oh, somewhere between three and four in the morning," Father answered cheerily. He winked at Alex.

Barbara groaned and sank into the nearest chair.

"May I ask what this family meeting is all about?" inquired Mother.

"It seems that we have had a visitor in our fireplace," Father told her.

"I did see him! I really did see him!" cried Rudy. He hopped across the room and pointed into the fireplace. "Right in there!"

"You mean you saw that jolly old elf, red suit, white beard, and all?" exclaimed Father.

"No, just his boots," Rudy admitted sadly.

"Oh, brother," sighed Barbara with a yawn.

Alex fumed. Just because Miss Mushy was thirteen and in middle school, she thought she knew everything!

"Well, it certainly looks like Santa Claus has been here," Mother said brightly.

"Yeah," Alex breathed excitedly. She had noticed that the stockings were overflowing and that there was a new softball bat leaning against the fireplace right under her stocking! "Can we look in our stockings?" she quickly asked.

Mother smiled and looked at Father. "I don't see why not," Father chuckled. "As long as we're up, we might as well do something important."

"Yippee!" Alex cried and bounded off the sofa. "Come on, Rudy!"

"Yeah!" The children raced to the fireplace and began pulling small treasures out of their stockings.

Alex found a giant candy cane and little pieces

of candy and stickers and a stuffed dog and baseball cards and felt-tipped markers and a poster of Garfield eating a pan full of lasagna. But the best thing of all was at the very bottom of her stocking—a brand-new softball. Alex loved softball. She was the star pitcher for her team, the Tornadoes.

"Dad," Alex cried when she pulled the softball out of her stocking, "Let's go outside and play catch!"

Her father laughed. "Now that would be just the thing to do at 3:30 in the morning in the snow!

"I have a better idea," he said after catching his breath. "Let's read about the very first Christmas."

Father waited until everyone gathered around him on the floor. He opened the Bible and began to read from the Gospel of Luke, "Now it came about in those days . . ."

A thrill went through Alex as she listened to her father read the story of Jesus' birth. Hearing that story always filled her with joy. It was not the same kind of joy that she felt from opening presents or from finding goodies in her stocking.

Those things were "outside" joys. Hearing God's Word was an "inside" joy. It came to her from God. That kind of joy began deep inside of her and grew until it filled every part of her.

Alex wiggled closer to her father. He was reading about the shepherds. That was one of her favorite parts. She didn't want to miss a single word.

Father read on about how an angel visited the shepherds and told them that Jesus had been born. The shepherds went to Bethlehem and found the baby Jesus just as the angel had said and the shepherds praised God for the gift of His Son.

Listening to the beautiful story of Jesus' birth made Alex feel that God was wrapping His arms around the whole world in a giant hug. She felt like hugging something, too. She grabbed the little stuffed dog that had come out of her stocking and squeezed it tight.

"Read about the Wise Men! Read about the Wise Men!" Rudy loudly begged his father.

Father turned to the Gospel of Matthew and read how the Wise Men came to Herod, the

wicked king, and told him that they had been following a star and asked the king if he could tell them where the Savior was born. King Herod sent the Wise Men to Bethlehem and told him to find the baby and then come back and tell him where the baby could be found.

The Wise Men went on to Bethlehem and found Jesus and Mary and Joseph. They worshiped Jesus and gave Him gifts of gold and frankincense and myrrh.

Father then read how the Wise Men were warned by God not to tell Herod where to find the baby Jesus, so the Wise Men went home a different way and did not return to King Herod.

Father closed the Bible.

"That's what Christmas is all about," Mother sighed peacefully.

"Yes," agreed Father. "Christmas is about loving, giving, and sharing. God loved us so much that He gave us His Son, Jesus. He wants us to share His love with other people." Father paused and then said, "Let's say a Christmas prayer."

The family joined their hands and bowed their heads. "Heavenly Father," prayed Alex's father, "thank you for sending your Son, Jesus, to be born into this world so many Christmases ago. Thank you for sharing Him with us. Show us how to give love to other people just as you give your love to us. Amen."

Alex suddenly thought about Eric Linden. Did God want her to give love even to Eric Linden? Brussels sprouts! Alex pushed away thoughts of Eric and their school project.

"It is now four o'clock in the morning," Father yawned. "What do you say to going back to bed for a few hours?''

"I think that's a wonderful idea," Mother quickly replied.

"Me, too," Barbara added.

Alex and Rudy did not agree. "We want to open presents now," they pleaded.

"Sorry, you're outnumbered," Mother told them. "Come on, up to bed, and I don't want to hear a peep until at least eight o'clock."

Everybody got to their feet and headed for the stairway. They all stopped suddenly. Rudy clutched Alex. A spooky howl echoed throughout the house!

CHAPTER 3

The Howl From the Basement

"What was that?" the children cried with fear in their eyes.

OW-OOO-ULLL!

Alex and Rudy grabbed their father's bathrobe. "What's going on?" Barbara exclaimed, moving closer to Mother.

"It's coming from the basement," Alex whispered.

OW-OW-OOO-ULLLL!

"Ahhh!" screamed Rudy. He tried climbing up his father's leg.

Alex pressed her face into her father's bathrobe and grabbed his leg tightly. She thought she felt her father trembling. Thinking that her father was so scared that he trembled, made Alex feel even more afraid. She looked up at his face. What? He was grinning! Father was trying his best not to laugh, but Alex could tell that at any moment he was going to explode with laughter.

Alex stepped back and put her hands on her hips. "All right, Dad, what's going on?"

That did it. Father collapsed into such a fit of laughter that he couldn't answer. Alex turned to ask her mother the same question, but her mother was in no better shape. Mother giggled and giggled until the tears rolled down her face.

Barbara, Alex, and Rudy stared at one another in surprise. Why were their parents laughing? Who was making that awful noise in the basement?

After a few minutes, Father and Mother reduced their whoops, hollers and giggles to low chuckles. "I'll go get our 'ghost' from the basement," Father announced.

Alex's eyes widened. She wasn't sure if she should be excited or scared. She decided she was both.

"What's Dad doing? Where's he going?" the children asked their mother as Father disappeared from the room.

"Wait and see," was all she answered.

They waited and listened. Father's footsteps were heard as he thumped down the basement steps. They heard his footsteps as he thumped back up. They strained to hear him pass through the family room and through the kitchen. When he got to the dining room, he stopped and peeked around the corner.

"Who wants to meet the howling ghost of the basement?" Father asked in a pretend spooky voice.

Rudy hid behind Mother. Alex took a couple of steps backward. Barbara held her breath.

Father grinned and stepped into the living room. He held up the "ghost."

"A puppy!" Barbara cried excitedly. In an instant, all three children ran forward, each trying to grab the puppy out of Father's arms.

The puppy was frightened with so many hands reaching for him and so many loud voices screaming in his ears. He buried his head in Father's arms and shook.

"Wait a minute! Wait a minute!" Father laughed. "He's afraid. See how scared he is?

Everybody calm down and you'll each get a chance to hold him.''

Father sat down in a chair and they all crowded around him.

"Where did he come from?'' Alex wanted to know.

"From the animal shelter,'' Father replied.

"Can we keep him?'' Rudy cried, jumping up and down in excitement.

"Yes,'' answered Mother with a smile. "He is our Christmas present to you and Alex and Barbara.''

"Oh, boy!'' hollered Rudy.

"I've always wanted a dog!'' Alex exclaimed. She was as happy and excited as Rudy.

"What kind of dog is he?'' asked Barbara.

"Well, I don't know for sure,'' Father laughed. "He's supposed to be mostly Labrador, but by the way he howls, he must have some hound in him.''

"We were hoping he would stay quiet until morning so we could surprise you on Christmas,'' Mother told them.

"Well, it is morning,'' Barbara pointed out.

"And it's Christmas," added Alex.

"And he sure was a surprise!" Rudy shouted.

They all laughed.

"May I hold him now?" asked Barbara.

Father passed the puppy to Barbara who snuggled him deep in her arms.

"He's the most beautiful puppy ever," Alex declared. She loved his velvety soft, black fur and his white nose with black freckles across it.

The loving strokes and attention made the puppy feel quite safe in his new home. He raised his head and cocked his ears at the faces all around. He barked a playful puppy bark.

Rudy turned a somersault and landed right side up a few inches from the puppy's nose. "Arf! Arf! Arf!" Rudy barked at the puppy.

"Arf!" the puppy replied.

Barbara put him down on the floor, and the puppy wiggled and bounced happily on his oversized puppy feet.

"He bit my finger!" Alex cried. "It didn't hurt," she quickly added.

Father and Mother watched as Barbara, Alex, Rudy, and the puppy frolicked together. The puppy especially liked to nip the children's bare toes as they scampered across the living room carpet on their hands and knees.

"Well," sighed Mother, "so much for sleeping."

"I don't think you'll ever get them back to bed now," Father observed.

"Oh!" Mother cried as the puppy suddenly discovered her slippers. He grabbed hold of one with his teeth and pulled. "Oh, dear, I was hoping he wouldn't chew on shoes," Mother frowned.

Father laughed at such a ridiculous idea.

After twenty minutes of rough and tumble, the puppy suddenly collapsed and fell sound asleep on his back. Two of his feet stuck straight up in the air.

"Awwww," Alex scooped him up in her arms and cuddled the soft, warm body next to her own. She lowered herself and the puppy to the floor and leaned back against a chair.

Everyone spoke in whispers as the puppy slept in Alex's arms. Alex closed her eyes. She didn't mean to close her eyes. They just closed on their own. She was very tired.

Later, Alex was startled to feel someone gently shake her arm. She squinted one eye open. The puppy was gone from her lap. "Hey," she mumbled.

"Come on, honey, the puppy's going to his bed and we are going to our beds," said Mother firmly. She pulled Alex to her feet.

Alex let her mother lead her up the stairs. She tumbled into bed and dreamed about a black puppy with white feet and a white nose covered with black freckles.

Alex woke to the sound of merry singing.

DECK THE HALLS WITH BOUGHS OF HOLLY,
FA LA LA LA LA, LA LA LA LA!
'TIS THE SEASON TO BE JOLLY,
FA LA LA LA LA, LA LA LA LA!

Alex sat up in bed. Her father's voice rang through the upstairs hallway. It was immediately joined by Mother's voice.

"Come on, Alex," cried Rudy, bouncing his way into her bedroom. "It's time to open presents!"

Alex leaped out of bed and rushed into the hallway. She and Rudy sang with their parents at the top of their voices.

Barbara soon struggled from her bedroom, looking half asleep. She, too, joined in the singing.

At a signal from Father, they all marched single file down the stairs to the living room. They sang as they marched.

This was the way Alex's family always greeted Christmas morning. Alex loved to sing Christmas carols while she followed her family down the big, curvy stairway. It was so exciting to see the lighted Christmas tree, surrounded by packages, waiting for them at the bottom of the stairs.

To Alex, it seemed as if the whole world was filled with merry music, twinkling lights, shiny presents, and happy people. She wished that this special moment would last forever. She was happy, and yet her happiness almost made her sad. In a few hours, the presents would be unwrapped, the company would come and go, the dinner would be eaten, and Christmas would be over. A shadow of a frown crossed Alex's face.

Her mother noticed. "What's the matter, honey?" she whispered to Alex.

"Oh, nothing, really," Alex sighed. "I guess I just want Christmas to last forever."

"So do I," her mother smiled.

Alex smiled back. It helped to know that someone understood. Alex turned to the pleasant task of opening Christmas presents.

Later, Rudy pranced around in his new astronaut outfit, a laser pistol in one hand and a teddy bear in the other. Shiny new cowboy boots completed his outfit.

"Alex, let's set up my new racetrack!" he shouted, bounding over to her.

"Watch out, Goblin," she hollered. Alex quickly jumped off a new pair of stilts before Rudy knocked into her. "Okay," she told him, "we'll put your racetrack together and then we will go outside and try out my new toboggan."

"Right," he agreed.

Alex spent the rest of the morning helping Rudy assemble his triple-spin, double-jump racetrack. The cars flew in upside-down loops and circles and jumped from one edge of the track to the other. Then, Alex and Rudy roared down Juniper Street in Alex's toboggan. It seemed to fly as fast as Rudy's race cars.

Later that afternoon, Alex's grandmas and grandpas, uncles, aunts, and cousins arrived. After Christmas dinner, they all gathered around the Christmas tree to sing Christmas carols. A new baby cousin, Jessica, lay on a blanket on the floor. She gurgled happily and grabbed her toes with tiny stubby fingers.

The family began singing "Away in a Manger." Alex didn't sing. Instead, she watched baby Jessica and found herself listening to the words of the song in a new way.

Away in a manger, no crib for a bed,
The little Lord Jesus lay down His sweet head.
The stars in the sky looked down where He lay,
The little Lord Jesus asleep on the hay.

"Brussels sprouts," Alex said to herself, "Jesus was really once a tiny baby like Jessica. But when Jesus was born, He didn't have a nice baby crib with lots of soft blankets. He probably didn't have any cuddly teddy bears to sleep with either. Why did God let His little Son be born in a smelly old stable with only prickly hay to sleep on? That doesn't seem right. Jesus was a more important baby than Jessica!"

As soon as the song ended, Alex asked her father, "Why was Jesus born in an old stable anyway?"

"Well, Firecracker, that's a good question," replied Father. "Do you think Jesus should have been born somewhere else?"

"Yeah, He is our King, so I think He should have been born in a palace," Alex decided.

"That makes sense from the way we see

things, Firecracker. But we don't always see things the way God sees them. God had Jesus born in a stable to teach us that it doesn't matter where a person is born or whether or not he is poor. What really matters is having God's love in our hearts. Jesus had God's love in His heart and He shared it with others. He loved people and helped people and healed people and taught them about God. He even died for them. Jesus wants us to share His love with other people.''

Alex thought about her father's words. She decided she would try her best to love and help other people just like Jesus.

CHAPTER 4

T-Bone in Danger

Their Christmas vacation passed quickly, and all too soon Alex and Janie hurried down Juniper Street's big hill on their way back to school.

"What do you think we'll do today?" Janie asked Alex.

"I don't know," Alex sighed. "I wish I could stay home one more day and play with T-Bone."

"T-Bone!" Janie laughed. "How did you ever think of such a name for your puppy?"

"Well, we all sat around thinking about dog names, like Rover and Fido, and nobody liked any of them. So we started naming things that dogs like to do and I thought of chewing bones. So I said we ought to name him 'Bones' and Dad said how about 'T-Bone,' and everybody liked that name. I think it's a great name!''

"Me, too," Janie agreed. "Hey! I wonder if we'll get to work on our projects today."

"Huh?" responded Alex. "Oh, yeah." Brussels sprouts! She wanted to forget about her project with Eric Linden.

"I hope so," Janie continued. "I think it's going to be fun."

"Maybe it will be fun for you, Janie," Alex retorted. "You have Julie as a partner. Think of me. I'm stuck with Eric Linden!"

"Yeah, that was pretty rotten luck." Janie gave her friend a sympathetic look.

Alex wondered. Was it rotten luck as Janie called it? Alex had been taught by her parents that there was no such thing as luck. Christians did not believe in luck! How could God let such a terrible thing happen to her?

That afternoon Mrs. Tuttle gave the class time to work on their projects. They all trooped into the library to use the encyclopedias.

Alex yanked the B volume off a shelf and smacked it down on a table in front of Eric. She plopped down beside him and quickly flipped through the pages until she found Brazil.

"Here," she said to Eric. "You copy that page and I'll copy this page." It was then that she noticed that Eric had brought nothing with him to the library—no paper and no pencil. Alex sighed and ripped a piece of paper out of her notebook, placing it in front of him. She grabbed an extra pencil and gave it to him. She started to work on her page.

After a few minutes, Alex glanced at Eric. He hadn't written down a single word! "Eric!" she exclaimed loudly. "Why aren't you working?"

Mrs. Tuttle heard her. The teacher walked over to their table. "What's the problem?" Mrs. Tuttle asked.

"I have written down half a page and he hasn't even started," Alex complained.

"Eric," Mrs. Tuttle gently reproached, "you are supposed to help Alex with this project. You are her partner. You cannot expect Alex to do all the work by herself."

"Right!" Alex exploded. "You want to get an F or something?"

Eric's face turned bright red. He slowly

reached for the pencil and began to write something down on his paper.

Mrs. Tuttle moved away.

Alex went back to her own paper. She felt rather bad about getting Eric in trouble with the teacher.

"Look, I'm sorry I got so mad," she apologized to him. "I didn't mean for Mrs. Tuttle to come over here."

Eric didn't answer. Alex shrugged her shoulders and got back to work.

Half an hour passed. Alex heaved a great sigh. She had finished copying the whole first page of the Brazil section in the encyclopedia. She had filled two pages in her notebook. She dropped her pencil and rubbed her aching fingers. She looked over at Eric. Brussels sprouts! He had written only one paragraph.

Alex gritted her teeth to keep from shouting out loud. This was never going to work. She was going to have to do it all by herself.

Just then a voice hissed behind her. "How's it going Whirlywind?"

Alex spun around in her chair. Eddie Thompson stood behind her, a smirky grin spread across his face. Eddie Thompson was always causing trouble. He called Alex "Whirlywind" to make her mad. Alex was a good softball pitcher and had struck out some of the boys in school ball games. Eddie Thompson was one of them.

Alex had a peculiar way of flipping her right arm over her shoulder in two fast circles before letting the ball fly over the plate. A teacher had once remarked that Alex looked like a regular whirlwind. To Alex's dismay, the boys in her class had picked up the nickname.

"Get out of here," Alex hissed back at Eddie.

"Hope you and Beetlehead have a good time together," Eddie sneered. He hurried away before Alex could punch him.

Eric's face was red again, even the tips of his ears. Alex felt sorry for him. Beetlehead was an even worse nickname than Whirlywind.

Alex raged, "Eddie Thompson's the meanest kid I know! Someone oughta stuff a bunch of worms in his big mouth!"

To Alex's surprise, Eric began to giggle. Alex giggled, too, as she pictured Eddie Thompson with a mouthful of worms. "Just think," she gasped between giggles, "every time Eddie opens his mouth to say something mean, a worm falls out!"

Eric laughed harder. So did Alex. They couldn't stop laughing. Their classmates stared at them. Mrs. Tuttle stared at them. The librarian stared at them.

Suddenly, the bell rang for afternoon recess. Mrs. Tuttle motioned for the children to leave the library.

Alex and Eric walked out of the room together. They walked out as friends.

That evening at dinner, Alex told her parents about Eddie Thompson and how she thought his mouth should be filled with worms because of all the mean things he said to other people.

"Oh, gross, Alex!" Barbara cried. "Please, not at the dinner table!"

"That reminds me of something in the Bible," Mother commented.

"There's something in the Bible about worms in your mouth?" Alex asked in amazement.

"Please," Barbara cried again. "I'm eating!"

Alex giggled. It was always great fun to disturb Miss Mushy.

"What I am remembering is not about worms," Mother went on, "but how a wicked tongue poisons the body. The Book of James tells us that our tongues can do great damage. Just as one little match can start a huge forest fire, so one little tongue can turn our lives into disaster."

"What do you mean like a forest fire?" Rudy asked with wide-opened eyes.

"Think of your tongue as a match, Steam Roller," Father told him. "Your little match tongue says something bad to another little match tongue. Then the second little match tongue tells the same bad thing to the third little match tongue. The third match tongue tells the fourth and the fourth tells the fifth and so on. Before you know it, the bad thing has spread to all the other match tongues just like a forest fire spreads from tree to tree until the whole forest burns down."

"Yuck," said Barbara, "that's awful."

"It is awful," Mother agreed. "We have to be careful and try to say only good things to other people. Otherwise, we will start forest fires with our tongues."

"Right," agreed Father, "and remember that the match that starts the fire also gets burned up in the fire."

After dinner, Alex told her mother how worried she was about the school project. "I don't think Eric's going to be much help," she complained. "He can't read very well and it took him a long time just to write down one paragraph when I wrote down two whole pages!" Alex folded her arms across her chest and scowled.

"Why don't you ask Eric to come home with you after school and you can work on your project here?" Mother suggested.

"Great idea!" Alex shouted. "Where's the school directory? I'll call him right now."

Alex rushed to the telephone and dialed Eric's number. After a few minutes of talking, she hung up the phone with a bang. "That Eric!" she stormed. "He hasn't even told his mother about our Brazil project."

"I'm not surprised," Mother replied. "Think about it in this way. When you have to do something that you can't do very well, do you like to talk about it?''

"No," answered Alex.

"That may be what school is like for Eric,''
Mother explained. "He might feel frustrated and
ashamed that he can't keep up with the other
children."

"Oh,'' Alex replied thoughtfully. "Kids are
always picking on him and calling him names
like Beetlehead."

"Sounds like he needs a friend.''

"Yeah, well, I'm trying to be his friend,'' Alex
declared, "But it's not easy."

"Usually, you will find that your most important tasks are not easy to do,'' Mother told her
with a smile.

The next day at school there was no time for the
children to work on their projects. At the end of
the day, Alex stood by Eric's desk and waited for
him to put his books and pencils away. He
seemed to be taking an extra long time in getting
ready to leave. Alex was getting awfully warm in
her coat and boots and mittens.

"Are you coming home with me?'' Alex
asked.

"Yeah." Eric closed his desk top with an extra loud bang. "My mom is making me!"

"Oh," Alex replied. She did not know what else to say. Eric threw on his jacket and followed her out the door. Janie was waiting for them outside.

The three of them trudged up Juniper Street's

long hill. It had snowed again the night before and the street was slippery.

The children were silent. Alex and Janie found it hard to talk with Eric stalking right behind them. Alex looked around for Rudy and Jason, but there was no sign of either one of them anywhere.

About halfway up the hill, Alex saw her brother. He was bending over Alex's new Christmas toboggan.

"That little goblin!" Alex screeched. "He's gonna get it!"

Just then Rudy straightened up and Alex could see a black bundle sitting in the front of the toboggan.

"Hey!" Alex shouted. "T-Bone is in the toboggan!"

Rudy grabbed hold of the back of the toboggan and pushed it and the puppy down the hill toward Alex and her friends. The toboggan quickly gained speed, flying down the street. The puppy looked terrified.

All at once, Rudy tripped and fell, letting go of the toboggan. It continued its downhill plunge, going faster and faster. Then, to Alex's horror, a car rounded the curve at the bottom of the hill. It started up the hill, heading straight for the toboggan and T-Bone!

CHAPTER 5

Runaway
Rudy

Every muscle in Alex's body froze in fear. It looked like her toboggan and her puppy and the car were going to collide in one big crash!

Janie covered her eyes and screamed. The scream jolted Eric into action. Like a streak of lightning, he dashed into the street and leaped onto the toboggan, forcing it to the side of the road.

Alex frantically waved her arms at the car and yelled, "Stop! Stop!"

Ice and snow flew from the car's tires as the driver slammed on the brakes. The car missed the toboggan by a few inches, spun in a half circle, and jerked to rest in a snowbank on the other side of the street.

For a long moment, Alex could not speak. She gazed at Eric sprawled on top of the toboggan. He had risked his life for her puppy by jumping in front of the car. She would never forget it.

The driver of the car awkwardly climbed out of his car onto a pile of snow. He stumbled off the pile and into the street.

"Are you kids all right?" he shouted at Alex.

Alex found her voice and shouted back, "I think so."

"You gave me an awful scare!" he told her.

"I'm sorry," Alex apologized. She tried to explain to the driver what had happened and pointed up the hill at Rudy.

Rudy sat in the street where he had fallen. His stocking cap tilted forward until it almost covered his nose. His jacket was torn wide open and one mitten lay on the ground behind him. He stared at them guiltily, like a robber caught in the act of stealing.

"Goblin, get outa the street!" Alex yelled. Rudy scuttled to the side of the road.

The driver returned to his car to dig it out of the snowbank. Alex moved over to stand beside Eric and the puppy. "Thanks for rescuing my dog," she said.

T-Bone whined and lunged out of Eric's arms into Alex's arms. They laughed. Alex hugged the whimpering black ball of fur.

"Whew, that was a close call," Janie declared, coming over to them. "You could have been killed!"

"No kidding," Alex snarled. She stared up the hill at her brother. "Rudy's going to get it," she muttered.

Alex handed T-Bone back to Eric and stomped up the street toward Rudy. Seeing the angry look on her face, Rudy began to back away.

"You are in trouble, Goblin," Alex growled.

"I didn't mean to! I didn't mean to!" cried Rudy.

"You almost killed T-Bone!" Alex screamed at him.

Rudy burst into loud wailings. A flood of tears poured from his eyes.

"I didn't mean to," he repeated.

"I don't care if you meant to or not!" Alex shouted in his ears. "It still happened! And

what's the big idea of using my toboggan?''

Rudy couldn't answer. He was too busy crying and choking on his tears.

"Don't you ever do that again, mush mouth!'' Alex warned. She heaved her brother into a snowdrift and motioned her friends to follow her into the house.

"Hold it, hold it; one at a time,'' Mother laughed, as Janie and Alex began telling Mother what had happened.

Mother began to frown. "Where is your brother?'' she asked Alex after she had heard the story.

"In a snowdrift,'' Alex jerked her thumb in that direction.

Mother sighed and went to put on her coat. "I'll get him,'' she called over her shoulder.

"Little brat,'' Alex grumbled. She and Janie began making hot chocolate. Soon Eric, Janie, and Alex happily sipped their drinks at the kitchen table. They recounted their dangerous adventure and congratulated Eric on his heroic leap to save T-Bone.

The front door banged open. "Alex?'' Mother called. "Which snowdrift?''

58

Alex stomped over to the front window. "That one," she pointed out the window.

"He is not there now," Mother told her.

"Maybe he buried himself underneath the snow," Janie suggested, skipping over to stand beside Alex.

Mother raised her eyebrows. "Who would ever do such a thing?"

"Rudy!" both Janie and Alex answered.

Mother nodded and went back outside. Eric joined Alex and Janie at the window. They watched Mother tromp across the street to the snowdrift. She poked at the snow. She soon straightened and loudly called Rudy's name.

"He must not be there," Janie said.

Alex shrugged. She was not going to spend any more time thinking about her brother. He had caused her enough trouble.

"Come on, Eric, we need to get going on our project," Alex decided.

Janie said good-bye and went home.

Alex pulled the B volume out of its place in the row of encyclopedias that lined a wall in the living room. She found pencils and paper and clunked it all on top of the kitchen table.

One look at Eric's face told her that he was not eager to start work on the project. She tried to think of a new way to make it more interesting. "Maybe we should try drawing a poster or something," she suggested.

Eric's eyes brightened at once. "What kind of a poster?" he asked.

"I don't know," Alex answered. "Let's look in the encyclopedia for some ideas."

They leafed through the pages. "Here's a flag and a soccer ball," Alex said as she stared at one page. "How good are you at drawing?" she asked Eric.

"It's my favorite thing to do," Eric declared. Then he frowned. "Some people think I draw too much."

"Who?" Alex wanted to know.

Eric shrugged. "My parents and Mrs. Tuttle."

"Why do they think that?" Alex asked.

"Well, they say I should be doing other stuff, like reading or math, instead of drawing all the time."

"Maybe you should," Alex replied.

"But I don't like doing all that other junk," Eric complained.

"Neither do I," Alex told him, "but I do it anyway so I won't be a dummy all my life."

Eric looked uncomfortable.

Alex changed the subject. "Can you draw this?" she asked, pointing to the flag.

"I think so," he answered. He quickly sketched on his paper.

Alex stared in amazement. The flag looked almost exactly like the picture in the encyclopedia.

"Brussels sprouts, that's really good," she exclaimed. "Now try the soccer ball."

Eric happily drew the soccer ball and then a Brazilian hat. Each one of his drawings was excellent. Alex praised them.

Suddenly a blast of cold air ripped through the kitchen. Mother, looking half frozen, stumbled through the door. "It is getting colder out there by the minute," she informed them, "and I cannot find your brother anywhere!"

"Aw, he's probably next door at Jason's," Alex told her.

"I have already checked there," Mother sighed. She sank to a kitchen chair, yanked her shoes off, and began rubbing her frozen feet. "I should have put my boots on," she admitted.

Alex watched a puddle ooze from her mother's shoes onto the kitchen floor.

"Look at these pictures," Alex told her mother. She shoved some paper under Mother's nose. "Eric drew all of them."

Mother looked at the drawings. "Eric, these are wonderful! Did you really draw them?"

"Yes," Eric answered shyly.

"Barbara ought to look at these drawings," Mother insisted.

"I ought to look at what drawings?" Barbara surprised them by suddenly appearing in the kitchen.

"Look at what Eric drew," Alex told her sister. She was as proud of his artwork as if she had drawn it herself.

Barbara held the pictures up close to examine them. "These are really good," she praised Eric. "Have you ever thought about going to art school?" she asked him.

"Art school?" Eric almost shouted. He looked as if he had never heard of such a thing.

"Sure," Barbara replied. "That's where I'm going to go someday. They teach you how to draw and paint and do sculpture and pottery and lots of neat things."

Eric whistled through his teeth.

"You see, when you get your art degree," Barbara continued, "you can spend your whole life drawing pictures or painting portraits or whatever you want to do."

Eric stared at her with wide eyes. He looked as if he had just discovered a dream come true.

"Of course," Mother added with a quick wink at Alex, "you have to get through grade school and middle school and high school first. They don't let people into art school until they can read and write and do math."

Eric did not say anything, but Alex could tell that he was thinking hard about art school. Alex turned to her sister. "We need to do a poster or something for our project. I was thinking about drawing a map, but maybe Eric should draw a bunch of pictures instead."

"Why not do both?" Barbara asked.

"Both?" Alex looked surprised.

"Sure," her sister urged. "You could draw a big, colorful map with pictures above it and below it."

"Great idea!" Alex shouted. "Don't you think so, Eric?"

"Yeah," he breathed, delighted with the idea of so much drawing and coloring.

For the rest of the afternoon, Eric and Alex planned their poster. They worked hard until Eric's mother came to get him.

"Bye, Eric, see you tomorrow," Alex called out the front door. As she watched Eric's car pull away, her father's car pulled into the driveway. Alex held the door open for her father.

"Thank you, Firecracker," said Father as he stomped through the door. He gave her a hug. "Brrrr! Tonight is supposed to be the coldest night we have had in January. I'm sure glad we are all inside!"

"We are not all inside," Mother told him as she entered the living room from the kitchen.

"Huh? What do you mean?" Father paused

while hanging up his coat.

"I mean, your son is outside somewhere in this freezing weather and I can't find him! I have called all of his friends and I have gone outside to look for him three times!" Mother looked like she might burst into tears.

Father put the empty hanger back into the closet and shrugged his coat on again. "I'll go look for him," he said. "It's almost dark out there."

By the time Father returned, it was completely dark. He had not found Rudy. He listened to Alex's story about T-Bone and the toboggan. He and Alex went outside to check the snowdrift one more time. Then, Father and Barbara went in the car to look for Rudy. Mother again called neighbors and friends. No one had seen Rudy.

Father and Barbara came home. Father shook his head at Mother as he stepped inside the door. This time Mother really did burst into tears. So did Barbara and Alex.

"Don't worry, we'll find him," Father tried to comfort them. He held Mother tightly in his arms. "I'm going to call the police," he told her.

CHAPTER 6

A Library Adventure

Alex stared out of the big, living room window. She loved to gaze out at the snow at night. It sparkled under the beam of the streetlight and filled the darkness with a soft beauty. But not tonight! Alex hated the snow tonight. It was cold and deadly and her little brother was lost in it!

Father, Mother, and Barbara sat in the living room with Alex. It was late, almost ten o'clock by the old grandfather clock, but nobody thought of going to bed. They were a family and they stayed together in times of trouble.

"I wish the police would call," stated Mother.

"I don't expect them to call until they have found Rudy," Father told Mother.

Alex continued to stare out the window. *What*

if the police can't find Rudy? she thought to herself. *What if he freezes to death? It will be all my fault. I'm the one who pushed him into the snowdrift.*

Tears began to run down Alex's face. She cried quietly at first, but soon painful sobs shook her body. She suddenly felt her father's arms lift her and carry her to the sofa. He held her close. Mother sat beside Father and patted Alex's back.

"It's my fault! It's my fault!" Alex choked between sobs.

"It's okay," soothed Mother.

"I didn't mean to make him run away," Alex declared through her tears.

"We know you didn't mean to," Mother told her.

Alex remembered Rudy had also cried "I didn't mean to" right before she threw him into the snowdrift. She wished that she had forgiven her brother the way her parents forgave her. If she had forgiven him, she wouldn't have thrown him into the snowdrift and he wouldn't be missing right now!

Father asked Barbara to sit on the sofa with

them. "Let's pray," he suggested. As they squeezed each other's hands, Father prayed, "Heavenly Father, we don't know where Rudy is, but you do. Please take care of him and bring him back to us. We pray in the name of Jesus. Amen."

The telephone rang. Father raced to answer it.

Mother, Barbara, and Alex followed him into the kitchen. They anxiously watched his face as he listened to someone talking on the other end of the telephone line.

"You found him!" Father cried joyfully. He grinned at Mother and the two girls. "Where?" he asked. "Kingswood High School? What is he doing at the high school?"

Father listened for a few more moments. "We will be right there to pick him up. Thank you, officer."

He hung up the telephone. "It seems that our son made his way to the high school where two custodians found him sitting by the front doors. They brought him inside and called the police. Rudy is now eating popcorn and drinking hot chocolate with the custodians!"

"Thank God," sighed Mother.

It did not take the family long to jump into the car and drive to the high school. When they reached it, they raced to the front door. Alex thought it was funny that her mother beat them all to the door. She couldn't remember ever seeing her mother run so fast!

"Thank you, Lord," was all Mother could say upon seeing Rudy wrapped in a blanket, safe and warm. She held him tight. Tears of joy flowed down her face.

Father shook hands with the custodians and thanked them for taking care of his son.

Alex stood by her mother and Rudy. There was something that she had to say to her brother. As soon as Rudy lifted his head from Mother's shoulder, Alex took a deep breath and said all in a rush, "I'm sorry, Goblin, for pushing you into the snowdrift."

"Aw, that's okay," he told her. "I had a real ad-ben-chure."

"You mean adventure," Alex corrected him.

Rudy shrugged his shoulders. "How is T-Bone?" he asked.

"He's fine. You want to go home and see him?" Alex asked.

"Yeah," Rudy wriggled out of Mother's arms and scampered to the front door, the blanket trailing behind him.

The family told the custodians good-bye and hurried through the cold to the car. Rudy sat in the front seat between Father and Mother. By the time they reached home, Rudy lay fast asleep, his head on Mother's lap. He was exhausted from his "ad-ben-ture."

The next morning the entire family slept late. Mother called the schools to explain why Barbara, Alex, and Rudy would be late.

Alex arrived at school just in time for the first recess. She told Janie and Eric and the rest of her friends about Rudy.

"You mean he walked all the way to the high school? That's a long way!" Janie sounded impressed.

Later that day, Alex and Eric sat in the library. Alex was writing the Brazil report. Eric was practicing his drawings and deciding how to arrange them on the poster. "We're going to need a big map," he said.

"There's one right here," Alex replied. She pointed to a page in the encyclopedia.

"No, that won't work," Eric told her. "It is too little. We need a bigger one."

"Hmmmmm." Alex thought for a moment. "I'll ask Mrs. Tuttle." She raised her hand. The teacher moved to their table.

"We need a bigger map of Brazil," Alex informed her. "Where can we get one?"

"You could go to the public library and look in an atlas," Mrs. Tuttle suggested.

"An atlas?"

"Yes, that's a book that has maps of all the countries in the world," Mrs. Tuttle explained.

"Are they big maps?" asked Eric.

"They are quite a bit bigger than encyclopedia maps," their teacher replied.

That afternoon Eric walked home with Alex, Janie, Rudy, and Jason. The older children teased Rudy on the way home.

"Rudy, how was your first day at high school?" laughed Janie.

"Oh, he doesn't go to school during the day.

He goes at night," Alex teased. "Did you know my brother is so smart that he decided to skip grade school and middle school and go right to high school?"

"Wow, Rudy, you will be famous," exclaimed Janie. "You'll be the first six-year-old high school student."

"I wonder if he'll make the football team?" grinned Eric.

"Cut it out, you guys!" Rudy stomped his feet.

When they reached home, Eric called his mother to tell her where he was. Alex told her mother that they had to get an atlas from the library.

"Alex, you cannot just get an atlas," said Mother. "You can't check them out of the library."

"Then how are we going to get a big map of Brazil?" Alex cried.

"There is a copy machine at the library. We can copy the pages we need," Mother told her.

Mother drove Alex and Eric to the library. "Where is an atlas?" Mother asked a lady behind the book checkout counter. The lady pointed Mother to a corner section of the library. Mother pulled an atlas off a shelf and handed it to Eric.

"Wow! Look at all these maps," Eric exclaimed.

"Find Brazil," Alex said excitedly.

"Here it is." Eric turned to a page. "And here is more of it," he said, turning to another page. "And more of it," he cried, turning the page again. "And more of it." He turned to the last page containing Brazil's map.

"Brazil is on four pages," Alex told her mother.

"I'm not surprised. Brazil's a big country," Mother replied. She looked around the library. "Now, where is that copy machine? I remember; it's in that little room over there." Mother pointed to another corner of the library.

"Alex," she said, "Eric and I will go back to the copy machine. You take this dollar and go to the counter and get me a dollar's worth of dimes."

"What for?" Alex wanted to know.

"For the copy machine. It costs a dime for each page that you copy, and I don't have any dimes."

"Oh." Alex ran to the counter.

"Shhhhh," a tired-looking woman behind the counter hissed. "There is no running allowed in the library."

"Oh! Sorry," Alex cried.

"Shhhhh," the librarian repeated. "We only use quiet voices in here."

Alex stared at the librarian for a moment. "Could I have some dimes, please?" she asked in a low whisper.

"What? I cannot hear you. What did you say?" the librarian asked crossly.

Alex gulped. She had been using her quiet voice like the librarian had told her to use. She said again in a louder whisper, "Could I have some dimes, please?"

"Well, why didn't you say so?" the woman snapped at Alex.

Some people at the nearest table had been listening to Alex and the librarian. They began to chuckle. The librarian frowned as she snatched Alex's dollar bill and handed her the dimes.

Alex plunked the dimes down on the counter to count them. "Ten, twenty, thirty, forty . . ." she counted out loud.

"What is the matter?" the librarian snapped. "Don't you think I gave you the right amount?"

"My mom always says to count my change," Alex told her.

The people at the table laughed again. The librarian folded her arms and began tapping her foot.

"Now, where was I?" Alex asked. "I better start over. Ten, twenty, thirty, forty, fifty, sixty, seventy, eighty, ninety, one hundred!" Cheers sounded from the people at the table as Alex finished counting.

"Uh, thank you," Alex told the now red-faced librarian. She tried to scoop the dimes off the counter into her hand, but in her hurry the dimes clattered noisily to the floor.

The people at the table jumped up and scurried in all directions to help Alex recover her dimes.

Within a few minutes, Alex held all of the runaway dimes in her hands. "Thank you," she cried to everyone and rushed to the copy room. She handed Mother the dimes and sank to the floor, breathing hard.

"Alex, what in the world has happened?" her mother asked. "What took you so long?"

"Brussels sprouts, you won't believe it!" Alex gasped. She told Mother and Eric about the librarian and the dimes.

"I don't believe it," Mother said when Alex had finished.

"I told you you wouldn't," laughed Alex.

Mother sighed and shook her head. She quickly made the copies of the Brazil map and drove them home.

CHAPTER 7

Falling Board Disaster

       Alex and Eric worked hard all week on their project. By Friday, they had decided which of Eric's drawings to use and where to place them around the outside of the map. Barbara showed them how to tape together the copies of the map.

"Now you can get some poster board and trace the map onto it," Barbara told them.

"Mom," Alex called to her mother in the kitchen, "we need to go get our poster board."

"Alex," Mother called back, "tomorrow's Saturday. Can't we wait until tomorrow to get it?"

"But, Mom, Eric won't be here tomorrow and he needs to go with us."

Mother sighed and looked at the clock. "I

guess I have time before dinner," she muttered.

When Mother entered the living room, she smiled. "You two have worked so hard on this project," Mother praised them. "I am proud of both of you."

"It's fun," Eric replied. "Look, I'll show you what we are going to do. This is where we want to put the flag—right up here. And here is where we are going to put the soccer ball." He began showing Mother all of his designs and plans for the poster.

Alex watched Eric explain their ideas to Mother. It was hard to believe that this was the same boy who never would talk to anyone. She remembered when she had first tried to talk to Eric. It had seemed impossible. And when he had first come to her house, he had hardly said a word. Now, he was talking and laughing with her mother as if she were his best friend! What had changed him?

Barbara and Rudy went with Mother, Alex, and Eric to the art store. Mother explained what they needed to the man behind the counter.

"I think you should get something heavier than

poster board," the man told Mother. "You need something sturdy for children to work on." He pulled out a thick piece of canvas stretched on a board. "This should hold up nicely and it comes in all sizes."

"Does it come as big as six feet by four feet?" Mother asked doubtfully.

The man whistled. "That is a big poster!" After a few minutes of searching, he found a piece the right size and carried it out to Mother's station wagon. He strained and pushed and tried his best to get the canvas board inside the back of the station wagon, but even with the seats down flat, several inches hung out the back.

Snow had already blown into the back of the car. "This won't work," Mother told him. "It's too cold and too dangerous for us to ride all the way home with the back door open."

"I'll tie it on top of your car," the man decided. He yanked the canvas out of the car and carried it back inside the store.

"I don't know if I like this idea or not," Mother worried. "I hope that board doesn't scratch the top of the car."

The man soon returned with the canvas board wrapped in plastic. He also carried a long rope. Piling the big board on top of the car, the man quickly tied it in place. "That ought to do it," he announced and hurried back inside the store.

"Well, here goes nothing," Mother sighed and started the engine. She slowly drove out of the parking lot and into the street. Everything seemed fine. The big canvas board rode smoothly on top of the car.

It wasn't until they were almost home that trouble began. The car was coasting down a long hill. At the bottom of the hill was a traffic light. The light was green but suddenly turned yellow a few feet before Mother reached the intersection. She slammed on the brakes. A rumbling noise sounded overhead. The canvas board broke loose from the rope and shot like a bullet down the windshield, over the hood of the car, and into the street!

Everyone held their breath as the board slid across the street and nearly hit a passing car. It bumped to a stop against the far curb.

"Brussels sprouts!" Alex gasped.

"Wow!" Eric exclaimed.

"Awesome!" Barbara breathed.

"Neato!" Rudy shouted.

"Oh, great!" Mother groaned and held her head. As soon as the light turned green, Mother drove across the street and parked the car by the curb where the board lay. The children piled out of the car to look at the board. Mother got out and inspected the top and hood of the car.

"I don't see any damage," she said, coming to stand by the children, "but it's too dark to tell."

"Now what do we do?" Barbara asked.

"We have to get our board out of the snow," Alex wailed. "It will be ruined!"

"Okay, okay," Mother muttered. "Just give me a minute to think. Do you think we could get this thing up on top again?" she asked Barbara.

Barbara shrugged. "We can try."

"Eric and I can help, too," Alex offered.

"Me, too," cried Rudy.

"Okay, let's try," decided Mother. "I will stand at this end of the board. Barbara will stand at the other end. Eric, you stand on one side of the board, and Alex, you and Rudy will stand on

81

the other side of the board. When I count to three, everybody lift."

They took their positions. "One, two, three!" Mother shouted. Everyone heaved and the board lifted into the air.

"This isn't so heavy," Alex said hopefully.

"You are not on the end," grumbled her sister.

"Everyone, move slowly to the car," Mother ordered.

They began moving to the car. Alex found herself walking backwards. Rudy, at her side, was also walking backwards. All at once, Rudy slipped in the snow and fell under the board!

"Aaaahhh!" he screamed.

"Rudy! Just stay there a minute!" shouted his mother.

But Rudy was making too much noise to hear her. He tried to stand up and bumped his head on the underside of the board, nearly knocking it out of their hands.

"Rudy! Stay still!" Mother shouted again.

Rudy sat down in the snow and howled.

"Good grief," muttered Mother.

Moving ever so slowly, the others managed to

move the board over Rudy's head. Eric nearly tripped over Rudy but kept his balance and his hold on the board.

When they finally reached the side of the car, Mother said, "Barbara, you and I are the only ones tall enough to reach the top of the car, so it's up to you and me to lift the board up there. Alex and Eric, you help lift as high as you can. Are we ready? Okay! Heave ho!"

They raised the board above their heads. Alex pushed upward as high as she could reach. So did Eric. Barbara and Mother tipped the board so that it was standing straight up in the air. They were ready to drop it onto the top of the car when a gust of wind whipped the board backwards, knocking it and Barbara and Mother to the ground!

"Oh, yuck!" Barbara screeched. She had landed in a puddle of wet, dirty slush.

Mother was not too happy either. "Any other bright ideas?" she asked sourly.

"Yeah," Alex piped up. "How about putting down the seats and putting the board in the back of the station wagon like the man from the store did?"

Mother did not reply right away. She stood up and brushed slush off her clothes. "I almost feel like leaving it here," she grumbled.

"Mom! You can't!" Alex cried. "What about our project?"

Mother rolled her eyes skyward. "All right, Alex, we will try your idea. Go put the seats down in the wagon."

Alex ran to obey. As soon as she collapsed the seats, she ran back to help the others load the board into the car.

"Okay, easy does it; guide it in there," Mother

directed. "Good, now tip it a little that way. I think we are going to make it this time."

With tugs and pushes, the board slid into the car as far as it would go. This time, nobody cared that it hung out the back of the car by a few inches. Mother tied the back door to the back fender with the rope.

Everyone piled into the front seat of the car. Alex sat on Barbara's lap and Rudy sat on Eric's.

"Well, things could have been worse," Mother commented as she started the engine. "The board could have hit another car when it slid into the street, or one of us could have been hurt trying to lift it to the top of the car."

"Or we might have had to leave it here," added Alex.

"I am glad we didn't have to do that," Mother smiled. "Now, let's go home and warm up!"

CHAPTER 8

A Prayer For Eric

"Hey, that's my mom's car," cried Eric as they pulled into the driveway. He pointed to a parked car.

"Oh, goodness," Mother replied anxiously. "I hope she hasn't been waiting too long."

As she drove into the garage, a door opened from the kitchen. "Back so soon?" joked Father.

Mother, Barbara, Alex, Rudy, and Eric stumbled out of the car. Father stared at their wet, slushy clothing and tired faces.

"What happened?" he asked.

"I'll tell you inside," promised Mother. "I don't think I will ever get my feet warm again!"

Eric's mother sat in the living room. When she saw them, she looked worried and relieved at the same time.

"Don't sit anywhere but on the floor," Mother told the children. "Excuse me," she said to Eric's mother. "We are all wet and cold. We had a little trouble bringing home a canvas board."

"I see," Eric's mother replied. "Is everyone all right?"

"Oh, yes, just cold," Mother smiled. She and the children explained what had happened to Father and Eric's mother. After hearing the story, Father went to the garage to get the board.

"This is heavy," he remarked, carrying it into the living room.

Alex and Eric quickly tore the plastic off of the board. "It's okay!" Alex cried in relief. "It's not wet or anything."

"Well, I guess I had better get Eric home," said his mother. She stood up to leave.

"Oh, please, wait just a minute," Mother cried. "I would like you to see the excellent drawings your son has made." She pointed to the taped-together version of the map still lying on the living room floor, surrounded by Eric's sketches.

"Yes, I noticed the map and the pictures,"

Eric's mom said. "I can tell that someone has worked hard on them."

"I helped some with the map," Alex told her, "but Eric drew all of the pictures."

"Really?" his mother looked surprised. "They are very good."

"We're impressed with Eric's artistic ability," Mother told her. "He has a real talent for drawing."

"Thank you," Eric's mother replied. "That is nice of you to say. I also think that Eric draws very well. The problem is that drawing is just about all Eric wants to do. His father and I believe that he should concentrate a little more on other things—homework, for example."

"This is homework," Alex quickly said.

"That is true," Eric's mother smiled. "If all homework was like this, Eric would do wonderfully."

Eric looked uncomfortable. Everybody was staring at him. "I just don't like all that other stuff," he mumbled. "I just want to draw."

"Brussels sprouts, Eric!" Alex exclaimed. "I don't always like to study either. I would rather play softball all day. But I don't. I do my math and reading and spelling because I know I have to. You don't want to grow up and not know how to read or add numbers, do you? People would really think you were dumb!''

"Ahem," Father cleared his throat. "Maybe Eric would agree to spend more time studying his school lessons in exchange for something he really wanted—like art lessons."

"Hmmmm," Eric's mother considered. "That is an idea."

"Aw, Dad would never let me take art lessons," Eric glowered. "He thinks art is a waste of time."

Eric's mother sighed and put her arm around her son. "Maybe your father thinks art is a waste of time because you spend all of your time drawing instead of doing your schoolwork."

Eric and his mother soon left. Alex, Barbara, Rudy, and Mother went upstairs to change into dry clothes. Father went to the kitchen to cook his specialty—grilled cheese sandwiches and soup.

Later when Mother came into Alex's room for bedtime prayers, Alex asked, "Mom, what did

Eric mean when he said his dad thought art was a waste of time?''

"Well, honey, sometimes it is hard for parents to recognize the talents that God gives to their children,'' Mother replied. "Eric's father may not see that Eric's art is a talent. He may see it more as a problem—something that Eric does instead of doing his schoolwork.''

"Eric ought to do his schoolwork first and then do his art,'' Alex decided.

"That sounds like a good idea to me,'' Mother agreed. "Even though it is important for Eric to develop his artistic talent, he also needs to understand that he has other responsibilities. We all have our favorite things to do, but we all have other things to do as well. I have to do laundry and clean the house and cook. Your father has to mow the lawn and clean the garage and take out the trash. You have to make your bed and clean your room and do your homework. We need to learn to balance our lives with things that we like to do and things that we have to do.''

Alex nodded. That made sense to her. "Do you think that if Eric starts doing well at school, his

father will like his art better?''

Mother smiled. ''I think there is a good chance of it. Why don't you put Eric in your prayers tonight?''

''Okay.'' Alex dropped to her knees beside the bed. Mother got down beside her.

"Dear Lord," Alex prayed, "please help Eric do good in school, and please help his dad see how good his art is. And please, Lord, make our project be really good so that Mrs. Tuttle will pick it for the Social Studies Fair. Amen."

The day finally came when Alex and Eric finished their poster. At least Alex thought so. Eric kept adding more things to it.

Below the map, Eric had drawn a giant soccer ball (Brazil's favorite sport). Below the soccer ball, at the very bottom of the map, he now added a compass. The compass read *"NORTE, SUL, ORIENTE, and OCCIDENTE,"* which meant north, south, east, and west in Portuguese, the native language of Brazil.

"Mom! Come and see! It's finished!" Alex yelled excitedly.

"Oh, it's beautiful!" Mother exclaimed upon entering the room. "Just beautiful."

"Fantastic!" Barbara added as she also came to inspect the completed poster.

Alex and Eric beamed. They were very proud. They had worked hard and the poster had turned out better than even they had imagined.

"Oh, I can't wait until tomorrow when Mrs. Tuttle sees it," Alex said. She and Eric grinned at each other. Tomorrow was the day that they would take the poster to school. Tomorrow was the day when their teacher would see it for the first time. Surely she would think it was the best poster. Surely she would pick it to represent the class at the Social Studies Fair.

The next morning Alex woke up early. She was too excited to sleep. She ran down the hall and into her parents' bedroom. She wanted to be sure her father did not oversleep. He had promised to drive her and the poster to school. If he slept too late, he would not have time to do it.

It was dark in her parents' room. Dark and quiet. Alex tiptoed to her father's side of the bed. "Dad," she whispered softly. He didn't move.

"Dad," she whispered again, a little louder. He still didn't move. She bent over and put her mouth next to his ear. "Dad!" she said in a loud whisper.

Her father sat straight up in bed. "What? What's wrong?" he mumbled.

"Uh, nothing," Alex replied, almost wishing she had not awakened him. "I mean, uh, don't you want to get up now? Remember, we have to load my poster in the car."

"Huh? Poster?" Father stared at her a moment, then peered at the clock beside the bed.

"Alex, for heaven's sake! It is four o'clock in the morning!" he exclaimed.

Mother was awake by now. "Alex, honey," she murmured, "it is too early to get up. Go back to bed."

"I can't sleep," Alex told her.

"Come on, Firecracker, we will see about that," said Father in a firm voice. He reached out and pulled Alex into the bed between himself and Mother. "Close your eyes and don't wiggle," he commanded.

With her father's arms around her she could not possibly wiggle. She didn't try. Before she knew it, she lay fast asleep.

BZZZZZZ!

Alex heard the alarm and felt one side of the mattress sink as her father rolled to its edge. She rolled down the mattress hill into his back. He switched off the alarm.

"Good morning, Firecracker," Father boomed in his usual, cheery morning voice.

"Hi, Dad," Alex responded. "Let's go load up the poster."

"Hold on," her father laughed. "I'm not even out of bed yet."

Before Alex had a chance to push him out of bed, Father got up and hurried to the bathroom.

Alex skipped to her room. This was the day! This was the day Mrs. Tuttle would see the project!

CHAPTER 9

Celebration

Father drove Alex, Rudy, and the poster to school. Alex patted her backpack. The written Brazil report was zipped safely inside it. She felt good about the report. She had gathered information about Brazil from two encyclopedias, a travel magazine, and a book from the public library. Mother had helped her organize the material. Alex had written the report very carefully—sometimes copying the same page over three times to make sure it was neat and all the words were spelled correctly.

Father unloaded the poster and carried it to Alex's classroom. Tingles of excitement ran up and down Alex. She could not wait to see Mrs. Tuttle's face when she saw the project. And what about her classmates? Wouldn't they be impressed to see such a gigantic poster?

Alex and Father turned into the door of her room. Alex grinned at her father. He winked and grinned back at her

"Here's Alex," someone yelled.

"Wow! Look at the size of that!" someone else shouted, pointing to the poster.

Mrs. Tuttle showed Father where to put the poster. "It is wonderful," she told Alex, "and so big."

"Come see my project, Alex." Janie pulled Alex over to where a large Japanese-style house stood outside the door. Inside the house, other dolls were seated on miniature pillows at a low table. Little bowls of rice sat on the table with a tiny pair of chopsticks beside each bowl. Miniature dragon pictures and colorful fans decorated the walls.

"Brussels sprouts," Alex gasped. "This is neat! What did you make the house out of?"

"Oh, my mom bought a kit and put it together," Janie answered proudly. "My mom also made the kimonos for the dolls. Aren't they cute?"

"Janie! You were supposed to make your project yourself," Alex reminded her.

"Well, Julie and I arranged the furniture and decorated the house," Janie said indignantly.

Alex shook her head. She thought of all the long hours she and Eric had spent working on their project. It was true that they had had some help. Barbara had helped them with ideas for designing the poster, and Mother had helped Alex organize the written report. But Alex had done all the writing and Eric had drawn all the pictures. It did not seem fair that all Janie had done was arrange furniture and hang up pictures!

Mrs. Tuttle gave the children time to inspect all the different projects. Standing beside Janie's Japanese house was a Canadian Indian village. Alex gazed at the Indians in canoes traveling past their teepees along a river made of aluminum foil. Beside the Indian village, a poster caught Alex's attention. It showed how an Egyptian pyramid was made. A gigantic pyramid constructed of papier-maché and sand sat beside it.

Alex walked about the room, studying each project carefully. She began to feel more and more uneasy. Now she was not so confident.

Alex moved past a group of boys. "Hey, Whirlywind, did you and Beetlehead smoke those cigars on your poster?" Eddie Thompson called to Alex. The boys snickered.

Alex turned and stared at Eddie. "Did you know that every time you say something mean, a worm falls out of your mouth?" she asked him.

"Huh?" Eddie looked shocked. He raised his hand to his mouth. The other boys laughed.

When Alex got home from school, she told her mother about the other projects and how she was worried that hers and Eric's project might not be picked for the Social Studies Fair.

"Now, Alex," her mother replied, "the other children deserve a chance. They worked hard on their projects, too."

"Not Janie!" Alex stormed. "Her mom put together a kit. That is not fair!"

"Well, I'm sure Mrs. Tuttle will be able to tell which children worked the hardest and which children did their own work."

"How?" Alex asked doubtfully.

"Oh, that is part of being a teacher," answered

Mother. "Mrs. Tuttle has lots of experience in judging projects. Don't worry about it," she added. "Be satisfied in knowing that you and Eric did your best. Now you have to leave it up to God and Mrs. Tuttle."

Alex considered her mother's words. She was right. They had done their best. There was nothing more they could do. She would let God and Mrs. Tuttle decide which was the best project.

The week went by slowly. Every day Alex went to school expecting Mrs. Tuttle to tell the class which project would go to the fair. Every day Mrs. Tuttle would tell the class that she had not quite decided. Tension in the classroom mounted. Mrs. Tuttle had to tell them soon. The Social Studies Fair was this coming weekend.

Finally, on Thursday morning, Mrs. Tuttle said, "I have decided which project should represent our class at the fair."

For once, the class was completely quiet. Not a rattle or a squeak or a whisper was heard.

"First, let me say that you have done a good job on your projects." Mrs. Tuttle smiled. "I am proud of all of you. There is one project, howev-

er, that stands above the rest. I can tell that the children who did that one worked extra hard."

Mrs. Tuttle paused. The children sat on the edges of their seats. Alex held her breath.

"The name of the country that will go to the Social Studies Fair is Brazil!" Mrs. Tuttle announced.

All the air that Alex had been holding back exploded out of her mouth in one big whoosh! "Brussels sprouts!" she gasped out loud. She quickly looked at Eric. He was grinning from ear to ear. She grinned back at him. The Social

Studies Fair! Their project was going to the Social Studies Fair!

After school, Alex ran all the way home to tell her mother the good news. Mother was so excited that she called Father. Father told Mother to forget about making dinner. He was going to take them out to dinner to celebrate. They would go anywhere that Alex wanted to go.

"That means pizza, right?" Barbara grinned at her younger sister.

"You bet," Alex replied. She licked her lips and pretended to taste hamburger, pepperoni, sausage, and gooey cheese.

That evening as the family feasted on pizza, Father said, "Well, Firecracker, I am certainly proud of you. Congratulations!"

"Thanks, Dad," Alex beamed. "Now I just hope we can win at the Social Studies Fair."

"Take one thing at a time," her father laughed. "This is a night to celebrate your project being chosen out of all the others in your class. We will think about the fair later."

"It was quite an honor to be chosen to go to the fair," her mother reminded her.

"That's for sure," Barbara agreed. "They have entries from every grade all the way up through middle school. It is really a big deal."

"Brussels sprouts," Alex gasped. It was exciting to think that she and Eric would be part of such a big event. Exciting and rather scary.

"And when does this big deal take place?" Father asked.

"Tomorrow night," Alex responded.

"Tomorrow night we take the poster and the written report up to the high school," Mother explained. "The judges will judge all the projects by noon on Saturday. After that, we can go see what they thought of Alex's and Eric's project.

"You mean I have to wait all the way until Saturday afternoon?" Alex complained.

"It's only two days away." Mother patted her hand.

"Seems like forever," grumbled Alex.

Her father laughed. "What does Eric think of all this?" he asked her.

"Oh, he is excited just like me," Alex answered. "You should have seen his face when Mrs. Tuttle told the class that she had picked our

103

project. He grinned so big that I thought his face might split open!"

Father laughed again.

"And he kept that grin on his face all day. Every time I looked at him he was grinning," Alex added.

"I am sure it meant a lot to Eric to have his project chosen," Mother said.

"Yeah, it is probably the first time something good has happened to him at school," Alex remarked. "I am really glad he was my partner."

"I remember when you were not so glad that he was your partner," Father reminded her.

"Yeah, I've been thinking about that. I mean, I wonder what changed Eric? He used to be so, uh, well, creepy. He would never talk to anyone."

Father and Mother smiled. "I think you played a big part in that change, Firecracker," said her father.

"Me?" Alex was puzzled.

"Yes, you gave Eric just the thing he needed to help him feel better about himself."

"I did? What did I give him?"

"Friendship," Father answered.

"Love," Mother added.

"God's love," Father stated.

Alex stared at her parents. Had she really given Eric all that?

"When you became a friend to Eric, you passed God's love to him," Mother explained.

"God's love! Remember, Dad? Remember on Christmas Eve when you said God wanted us to share His love with other people?"

"I sure do," Father smiled.

"Well, when you said that, I thought of Eric. Only then, I didn't like him and I didn't want to think about sharing God's love with him. I guess God really did choose Eric to be my partner! When Mrs. Tuttle first called out our partners for our projects, I prayed that God would choose a good partner for me. And He did. He really did. I just didn't know it then."

Her parents laughed.

"That is an important thing to understand about God, Alex," her mother said. "God looks ahead. He has a purpose for everything that happens to us. And His purpose is always good. We just have to believe that whatever God lets happen to us is for our good."

"And remember this, Firecracker," her father added. "God's specialty is miracles. The more impossible something seems to us, the bigger the miracle God can do."

"Like Eric becoming my friend and our project getting chosen!" Alex exclaimed. A flood of love and joy swept through her. Here was another inside joy. The joy of knowing that God cared about every part of her life and that she, Alex, had actually shared His love with another person.

CHAPTER 10

The Greater Prize

Friday dragged on and on and on. Every time Alex glanced at the clock on the classroom wall, it had only moved a few minutes. Would the day never end? She could hardly wait for her father to pick up the poster and take it to the high school. She and Eric were going to go with him. Mother and Eric's parents were going to meet them there.

At ten minutes after three, Alex saw her father waiting in the hallway outside the classroom door. "Oh, hurry up," Alex told the clock silently. "Hurry up and race through the last five minutes."

The last bell finally rang and Alex let out a loud "Whoopee!" The other children laughed. Mrs. Tuttle smiled. They all knew how important this day was to Alex and Eric.

Even though the last bell had rung, no one left the classroom. The children wanted to see the project safely loaded into Alex's car. After all, the project would represent their class at the Social Studies Fair.

In Alex's opinion, Father took much too long to get the poster out of the classroom. First he had to talk with Mrs. Tuttle. Then he had to joke and laugh with the other children. Alex reminded him at least ten times that they had better be going.

Finally, with a parade of children behind him, Father carried the poster to the car. He shoved it into the back of the station wagon. Alex and Eric jumped into the front seat.

"Good-bye, Alex," Janie called through the front window. "My mom and I are coming to see your project tomorrow at the high school. I hope it wins first prize!"

"Thanks, Janie," Alex called back. She was glad that Janie was not mad because her project was chosen instead of Janie's. Janie was a good best friend.

When they reached the high school, Father

groaned to see a double line of cars stretched all around the circular driveway at the front entrance. The cars were moving, but very slowly. Whenever a car reached the big front doors, it would stop and people would jump out to unload their projects.

"They certainly need a better system than this," Father observed.

"Dad," Alex said worriedly, "we only have until seven o'clock to get our project in there."

Father looked at her with raised eyebrows. "Firecracker, I believe we have plenty of time. It will not be seven o'clock for three more hours!"

After what seemed like more than three hours to Alex, their car reached the front doors. "All out!" Father ordered.

Alex could see her mother standing just inside the double doors. She was talking to a man and a woman next to her.

"There's your mom," Alex told Eric. "Is that your dad next to her?"

"Yes," he answered excitedly.

Mother spotted them and pointed. Eric's father rushed out the front door.

"Here, let me help you," he offered. He grabbed an end of the poster and helped Father carry it inside. Alex and Eric ran behind them.

"Thank you," Father told Eric's father. They stood the heavy poster against a near wall. Father hurried back outside to move the car out of the driveway.

Alex gazed around in amazement. Crowds of people moved through the hallways carrying posters, statues, models, and paintings. She gasped when two boys passed her toting a large wooden castle.

"So this is the poster," Alex heard Eric's father say.

"Yes," Eric replied.

"Did you draw all of those pictures?" his father asked.

"Yes," Eric answered.

"They are very good," his father said.

"He drew all of them, even the bananas!" Alex told Eric's father. "I helped color things like the big ocean."

"They have worked hours and hours on this project," Mother remarked.

"I can tell that they have," Eric's father replied. "It is a wonderful poster." He patted his son's shoulder.

Just then Father returned from the parking lot. "Boy, is it ever a mess out there! I circled the parking lot twice before I found a place to park."

"Where do we take the poster?" Eric's father asked.

"Mrs. Tuttle said to put it in the gym," Alex replied.

"That's right," said Mother. "We're supposed to set it up in the third-grade section."

"Okay, let's go find the gym," Father said. He and Eric's father lifted the poster once again and started down the hallway.

"It's here! The gym's right here!" Alex yelled down the hallway to the grown-ups. She and Eric had skipped ahead of the others.

"Brussels sprouts!" Alex gasped as she peeked inside the crowded room. A long row of tables, stretching the entire length of the gym, stood a few feet from the door. Above the tables hung signs—"1st, 2nd, 3rd"—all the way to "8th." Behind the tables stretched row after row

111

after row of projects. The projects sat or leaned against other tables.

Alex and Eric stared at one another. To them it looked like all the projects ever made in the world were inside that gym.

The grown-ups caught up to Alex and Eric and they moved to the table marked "3rd."

"Yes, we have your names right here," a woman behind the table told Mother. "Please take your project to an empty spot in one of the rows behind me. Here are your name tags. Attach them to the table in front of your project." She handed Mother a roll of tape from a stack on the table in front of her.

Alex and Eric led the way down a row. The mothers followed. The fathers came last, tipping and turning the poster to avoid hitting other people. They found an empty spot and stood the poster up. Alex set the written report beside it on a table. Mother taped their name tags to the table.

"Well, I guess that's all we have to do," Mother said.

"Yes, I would say this is it until tomorrow," agreed Father.

"Do you want to stay awhile and look around?" Eric's mother asked.

"No!" Eric and Alex answered together. They did not care to see any of the other projects. It would only make them worry.

"Then, let's go home," Father suggested.

As Alex walked toward the door, she glanced back at the poster. It had been such a big part of her life for the last few weeks that she did not want to leave it there all by itself. But there was nothing else she could do. Again, she would have to leave it up to God and the judges, just as she had left it up to God and Mrs. Tuttle.

"Don't worry, Eric," Alex whispered. "God will make sure that the right project gets picked. And you know what? I think ours is the right project!"

"You really think so?" Eric whispered back.

"You bet! Come on, I'll race you down the hall!"

Before any grown-up could stop them, the children sped down the hallway, leaving their worries behind!

The next day, Alex and her family met Eric and

his parents at the front doors of the high school. Eric quickly pulled Alex to one side, away from everyone else.

"Guess what!" he exclaimed.

"What?" Alex asked.

"My dad said that if I bring my grades up in math and reading, he will let me take art lessons!"

"That is fantastic!" Alex shouted. She grabbed his hands and swung around in a circle.

"Are you two about ready to go see how they judged your project?" Father called to Alex and Eric.

Alex and Eric stopped whirling. They looked at each other. This was the big moment. Were they ready? Taking deep breaths, they both answered, "Yes!"

At the door to the gym Alex asked, "Can Eric and I go in alone first? You see, it's sort of special just to us."

"Of course you can," Mother told them. "We will wait right here until you tell us to come in."

Alex and Eric made their way around people and down the rows to their project. They stopped a few feet away from it. Their faces lit up with surprise. Alex rushed to the table. Eric leaped straight into the air. Suddenly, both children were shrieking at their parents, waving blue ribbons and trophies!

"They did it!" cried Father.

"Thank you, Lord," praised Mother.

The grown-ups, Barbara, and Rudy rushed across the room to Alex and Eric. Everyone hugged and shouted and laughed at the same time. The mothers wiped happy tears from their eyes.

"I knew you could do it, Short Stuff," Barbara told her sister with a squeeze. That was one squeeze Alex did not try to wriggle out of. It was good to know that her big sister was proud of her.

The rest of the afternoon was one big blur of excitement for Alex. She and Eric had their pictures taken on a stage at the back of the gym. They held up their trophies and ribbons and grinned at the photographer. Mrs. Tuttle and Janie and several other classmates came to share their happiness.

All in all, it was a glorious day. When it was

over, Alex said good-bye to Eric and his parents.

"Alex," Eric said rather shyly, "now that the project is over, can we still be friends?"

"Of course," Alex replied. "We *are* friends. Not just project friends, but real friends."

Alex watched Eric walk away with his parents. *It's true,* she thought, *we are real friends. And even if we hadn't won our trophies today, we would still be friends.*

Alex looked down at the trophy in her hand. All at once, she realized that it was not so important. That surprised her. She had considered winning first prize the most important thing she could do. But she had been wrong. Winning Eric's friendship was more important. That was the greater prize.

"Well, Firecracker," her father boomed as they walked to the car. "This was certainly a grand day. I almost hate to see it end."

His words suddenly made Alex remember Christmas Day and how she had felt sad to think of that day ending. "But Christmas doesn't really end," she told herself, "because Jesus never ends. And today won't really end either because

Eric and I will always be friends."

Alex looked up at her father. "Don't worry, Dad," she told him. "Today won't really end because I have something important to remember it by that will last a long time."

"What's that, Firecracker, your trophy?" Father asked.

"No," Alex grinned. "Eric's friendship!"

Amen.

SHOELACES AND BRUSSELS SPROUTS

One little lie, but BIG trouble!

When Alex lies to her mom about losing her shoelaces, it doesn't seem like a big deal. But how do you replace special baseball laces when you don't have any money and you're not allowed to go to the store alone? A big softball game is coming up, and Alex knows the coach won't let her pitch in shoes without laces—or in cowboy boots!

Every kid gets into the predicaments that Alex does—ones that start out small and mushroom. Readers will learn from Alex's mistakes and understand that they have the same sources of help that she turns to: A God who loves them and wants to help them, and parents who understand.

Other books in the Alex Series . . .

2 *French Fry Forgiveness*—Sometimes making friends is harder than making enemies.

3 *Hot Chocolate Friendship*—Is winning first place as important to Alex as being a friend?

4 *Peanut Butter and Jelly Secrets*—Obeying her parents (even in little things) beats the awful results of disobeying.

PEANUT BUTTER AND JELLY SECRETS

Where did her money go?

Alex's mom *trusted* her with her school lunch money—and now it's gone! How will she ever get through the week without Mom *or* her teacher finding out? And what will she do when her class goes to lunch for the next five days?

Every kid gets into the predicaments that Alex does—ones that start out small and mushroom. Readers will learn from Alex's mistakes and understand that they have the same sources of help that she turns to: A God who loves them and wants to help them, and parents who understand.

Other books in the Alex Series . . .

1 *Shoelaces and Brussels Sprouts*—It's always better to tell the truth, as Alex learns the hard way.

2 *French Fry Forgiveness*—Sometimes making friends is harder than making enemies.

3 *Hot Chocolate Friendship*—Is winning first place as important to Alex as being a friend?